FOR
snodgRASS
aND THE
FISH
(those TWO FAMOUS GRiNNeRS)

For games, fun activities and to find out more about the illustrator, visit:
www.wonkybutton.com

ORCHARD BOOKS
338 Euston Road, London NW1 3BH

Orchard Books Australia
Level 17/207, Kent Street, Sydney, NSW 2000

First published in 2009 by Orchard Books
First published in paperback in 2009
Text and illustrations copyright © Leigh Hodgkinson 2009

The right of Leigh Hodgkinson to be identified as the author and illustrator of this work has been asserted by her in accordance with the Copyright, Designs and Patents Act, 1988.

A CIP catalogue record for this book is available from the British Library.

ISBN 978 1 40830 182 1
10 9 8 7 6 5 4 3 2 1
Printed in China

Orchard Books is a division of Hachette Children's Books, an Hachette UK company.

www.hachette.co.uk

smile!

Leigh Hodgkinson

ORCHARD BOOKS

Mum says I am to have NO MORE biscuits before tea time. (And that includes CRUMBS and broken bits.)

By the way, I am DEFINITELY NOT sulking.

I am NOT particularly chipper or CHiRPY either. Usually **THESE** things are ME in a nutshell, but not today. This is because I've just realised something

TERRIBLE!

I have LOST something V e R y
<u>VERY</u> IMPORTANT.
The thing I have LOST is my SMILE.
I wish I could find it.

If I had my smile, everything would
be very nice and normal indeed.

You see, I **LOVE** to smile!
Smiling is one of my favourite hobbies.
Smiling makes me feel SUNSHINEY
and as fresh as a daisy,
<u>WHATEVER</u> the weather!

SPLOSH!

My dad (who must be on his way to the moon) says I should try to REMEMBER where I last saw it.

And I think,
RIDICULOUS!
If I knew THAT, then it wouldn't be LOST, would it?

Dad says I will just have to look for it.

BUT looking for things is <u>SO BORING</u>.
IF I was a MULTI-EYED ALIEN,
finding lost things would be SUPER speedy.
I'm not a MULTI-EYED ALIEN though.

I'm just me.

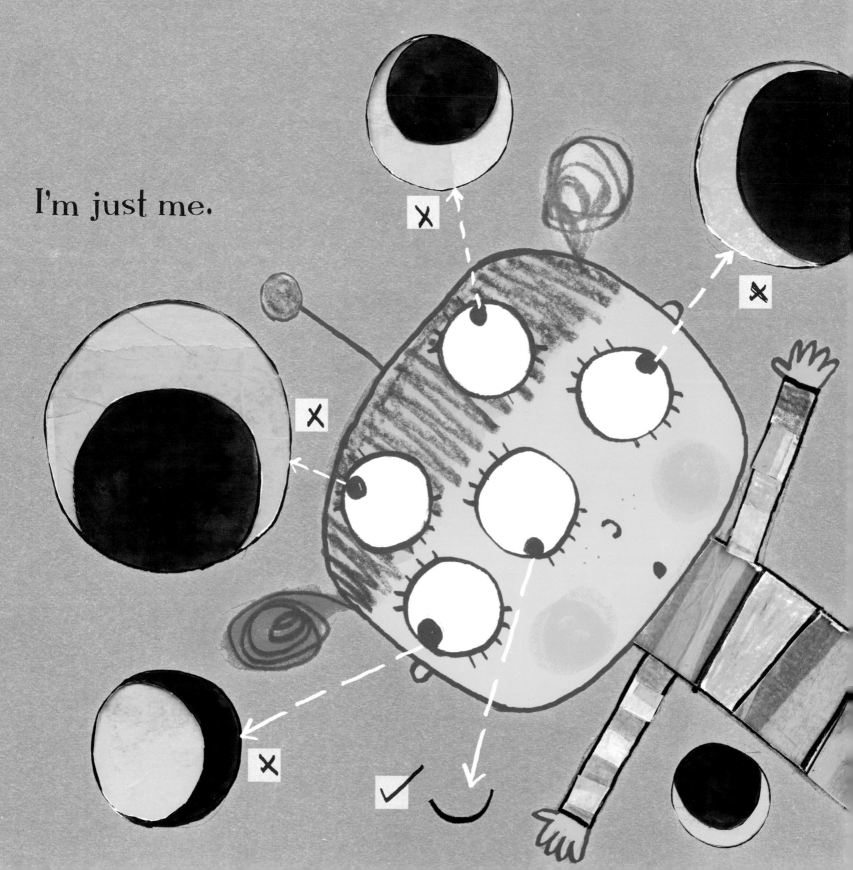

Maybe my smile has fallen
under my bed.
So I LOOK, but it ISN'T there!
(Even though

EVERYTHING

else seems to be.)

Perhaps I dropped it on the FLOOR?
If there IS a floor under all this stuff!
I don't think I have ever seen it.
It COULD be an ocean made of
WIBBLY WOBBLY JELLY
for all I know.

RASPBERRY
JELLYFISH

I suppose I had better TIDY UP.
This is HIGHLY UNUSUAL,
but I'm DESPERATE!

doggy PADDLE

No smile to report here.

Only one UN-higgledy-piggledy

bedroom and NO jelly.

But what if I didn't LOSE my smile?
What if SOMEBODY took it?

Well, I don't think it was Glittergills.

Cheer up,
Glittergills!

Maybe a sprinkle of fishy-flakes will do the trick?

AHA!

Maybe the TWINS took it?
They ask me what I'm up to,
so I tell them – and they just
giggle.

However, I don't think they're to blame (this time) as their smiles are much **BIGGER** than mine and MUCH more ANNOYING.

MY smile is EXACTLY the right shape and size for

just me!

It simply wouldn't suit **ANYBODY** else.

So, if it ISN'T in my bedroom and it HASN'T been stolen . . .

it must be LOST in the
BIG WIDE WORLD.

But it will take **AGES**
to look there . . .

Maybe I'll quickly check
the rest of our house first.

Mum says that **MOST** lost things in this house can be found in the following places:

1. The sofa

2. Pocket

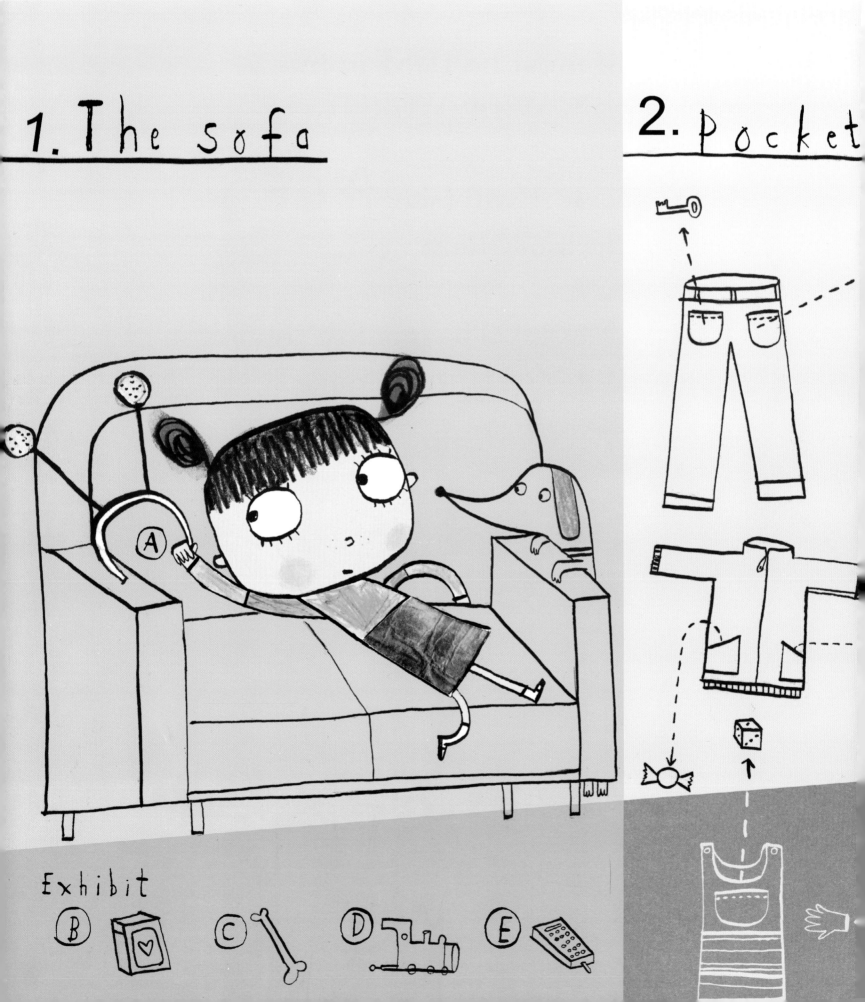

Exhibit

3. MR HONEYCOMB'S basket

Oh look!
One of Dad's **FLIP-FLOP**s.

(I think this is the **FLOP** one.)

tHe DOG HOUSE

Well, seeing as I am here, I'll just have a quick game with Mr Honeycomb.

(He is **ONE** smart cookie!)

tHe DOG HOUSE

FIVE games later,
Mum finds me and says that
my SPICK -and- SPAN
room is a COMPLETE
miracle!
She ALSO says that I am
a SWEET PEA for feeding
Glittergills and playing with
Mr Honeycomb.

I think

MR HONEYCOMB

agrees!

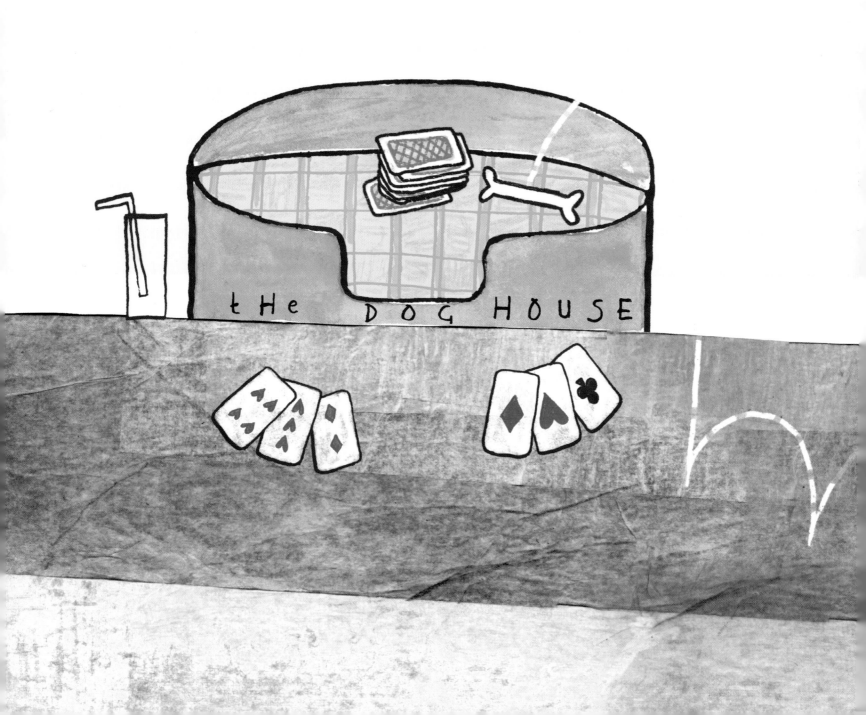

"You've found it then!"
say the twins.

And I say, "FOUND WHAT?"

"We KNEW it would turn up!" say the twins.

And I say, "Knew **WHAT** WOULD TURN **UP**?"

and THEY say . . .

Smiling.